WE ARE Water PROTECTORS

Written by
Carole Lindstrom

Illustrated by
Michaela Goade

To Dan and Sam. And to water protectors everywhere — C. L.

For Mother Earth and all who defend her — M. G.

Text copyright © 2020 by Carole Lindstrom
Illustrations copyright © 2020 by Michaela Goade
Published by Roaring Brook Press
Roaring Brook Press is a division of Holtzbrinck Publishing Holdings Limited Partnership
120 Broadway, New York, NY 10271
mackids.com

Library of Congress Control Number: 2019941023
ISBN: 978-1-250-20355-7

Our books may be purchased in bulk for promotional, educational, or business use. Please contact your local bookseller or the Macmillan Corporate and Premium Sales Department at (800) 221-7945 ext. 5442 or by email at MacmillanSpecialMarkets@macmillan.com.

First edition, 2020
Book design by Aram Kim
Printed in the United States of America by Worzalla, Stevens Point, Wisconsin

10 9

WE ARE Water PROTECTORS

Written by
Carole Lindstrom

Illustrated by
Michaela Goade

ROARING BROOK PRESS
NEW YORK

Water is the first medicine, Nokomis told me.

We come from water.

It nourished us inside our mother's body.

As it nourishes us here on Mother Earth.

Water is sacred, she said.

We stand

With our songs

And our drums.

We are still here.

The river's rhythm runs through my veins.

Runs through my people's veins.

My people talk of a black snake that will destroy the land.

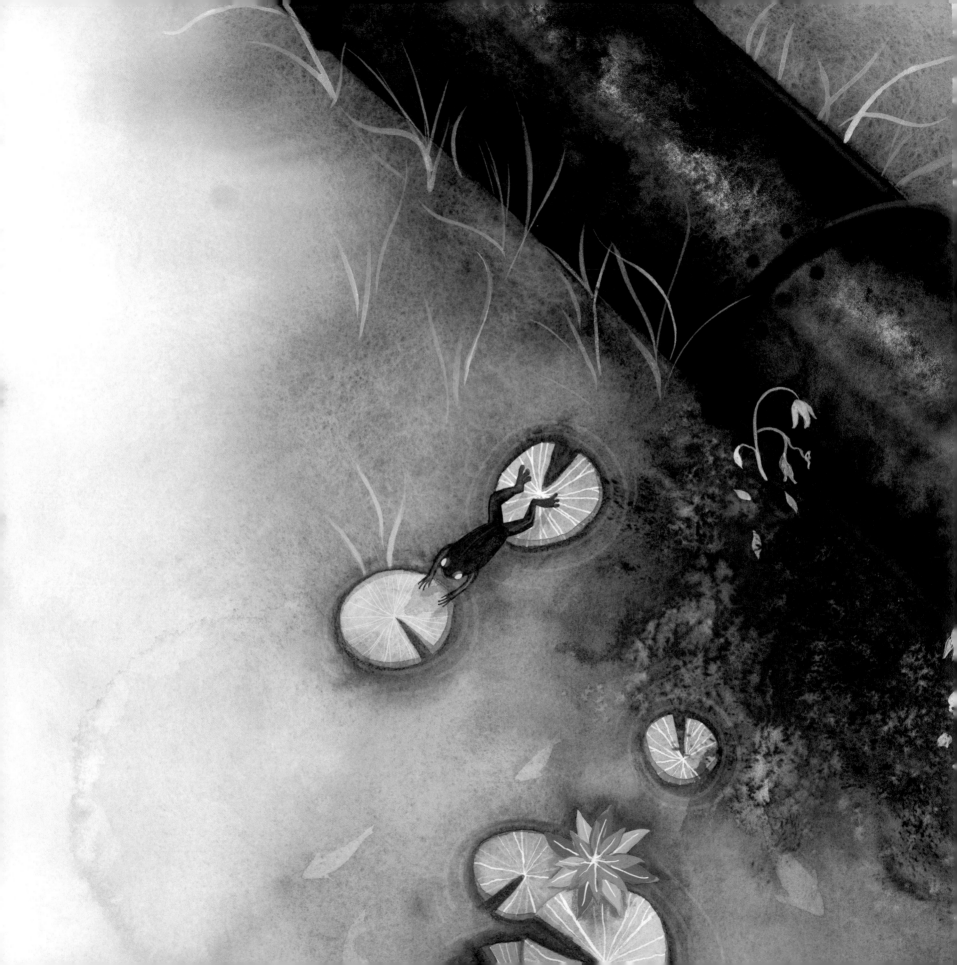

Spoil the water.
Poison plants and animals.
Wreck everything in its path.

When my people first spoke
Of the black snake,
They foretold that it wouldn't come
For many, many years.

Now the black snake is here.

Its venom burns the land.

Courses through the water,

Making it unfit to drink.

TAKE COURAGE!

I must keep the black snake away

From my village's water.

I must rally my people together.

To stand for the water.

To stand for the land.

To stand as ONE.

Against the black snake.

We stand

With our songs

And our drums.

We are still here.

It will not be easy.

We fight for those
Who cannot fight for themselves:
The winged ones,
The crawling ones,

The four-legged,

The two-legged,

The plants, trees, rivers, lakes,

Tears like waterfalls stream down.

Tracks down my face.

Tracks down my people's faces.

Water has its own spirit,

Nokomis told me.

Water is alive.

Water remembers our ancestors

Who came before us, she said.

We stand

With our songs

And our drums.

We are still here.

We are stewards of the Earth.
Our spirits have not been broken.

We are water protectors.

WE STAND!

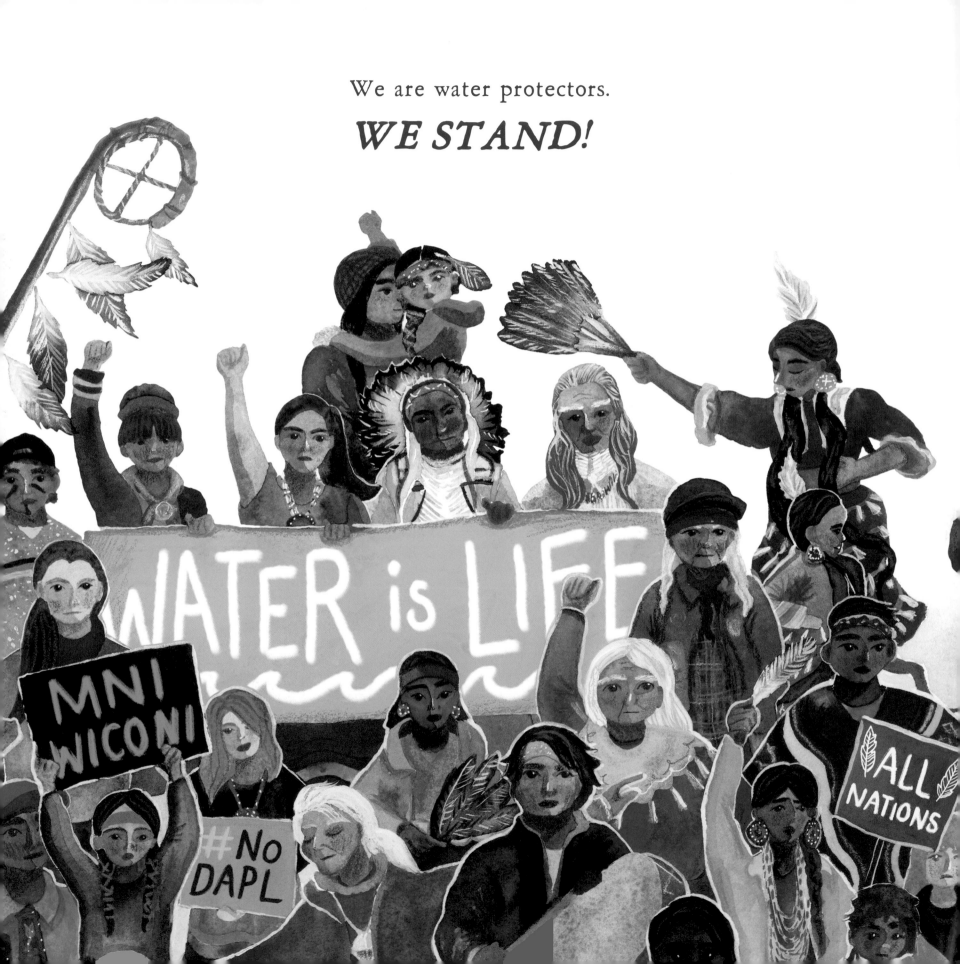

The black snake is in for the fight of its life.

MORE ON WATER PROTECTORS

*I*n Ojibwe culture, women are the protectors of the water and men are the protectors of the fire. Perhaps it is for that reason that I felt compelled to speak for the water through this story. Humans have been mistreating Mother Earth for millennia, and Indigenous Peoples have long acted as stewards of the planet, giving a voice to our silent home.

There is an Anishinaabe prophecy that speaks of two roads: One road is a natural path. It leads to global peace and unity that embraces the sacred relationship between humanity and all living things. On this path, all orders of creation—mineral, plant, animal, and human—are relatives deserving of respect and care. We are instructed to use our voices to speak for those who have not been given a voice. On this path there is no "black snake." The Earth is not damaged, and the grass grows lush and green.

This prophecy, known as the Seven Fires Prophecy, says that if humans choose the natural path, then we will proceed toward peace and unity and a healthy Mother Earth.

The other road is described as a hard-surfaced highway where everything moves faster and faster, at an unimaginable speed. On this path, humans embrace technological advancement with little regard for Mother Earth.

Many Native Nations believe this path is symbolized by the oil pipelines, the "black snakes" that crisscross our lands, bringing destruction and harm. This path leads to a damaged Earth.

The prophecy is coming to life right before our eyes.

This book was created as I became increasingly aware of the many tribal nations that are fighting oil pipelines from crossing their tribal lands and waterways.

In April 2016, the Standing Rock Sioux Tribe stood up against the titans of industry to protect their region's water and sacred burial grounds from one of these oil pipelines—the Dakota Access Pipeline (DAPL).

Although the tribes and residents are often told that these pipelines are safe, there are countless oil leaks every year across the world. These leaks cause tremendous damage and destruction to plants, wildlife, and water.

What started out as a camp made up of a few tribal members near the Cannonball River in Fort Yates, North Dakota, would eventually grow into a movement that would bring together more than five hundred Indigenous Nations from all over the world to stand for clean water.

Seeing reports of the protests had a profound effect on me. I am a citizen of the Turtle Mountain Band of Ojibwe, a tribe also located in North Dakota. While other members of my tribe traveled to Standing Rock to lend their support, traveling to North Dakota from my home in Maryland wasn't possible for me at the time. But I knew what was! Using my voice to tell a story. A story to honor the Standing Rock Water Protectors and share this historical movement with the world. Sadly, despite the fierce protests, construction of the Dakota Access Pipeline moved forward—with no assurances to the Standing Rock Sioux Tribe that the pipeline wouldn't leak and that their water sources would be safe from contamination. Unfortunately, there were leaks in the Dakota Access Pipeline before construction was even complete.

Like the Standing Rock Sioux, many tribes and their allies continue to fight pipelines on a daily basis.

This is not just a Native American issue; this is a humanitarian issue. It is time that we all become stewards of our planet so we can protect it for our children and our children's children.

Water affects and connects us all. We must fight to protect it.

I have hope that the next generation, YOU, will continue to see the importance of preserving our precious planet by pledging to be a Water Protector with me!

Aapiji go miigwech.

Your niiji,
Carole

FURTHER READING

The Mishomis Book: The Voice of the Ojibway by Edward Benton-Banai

GLOSSARY

Anishinaabe [ah-nish-eh-nah-BAY]: The people. It refers to the three tribes of the Council Fires, or the People of Three Fires—Ojibwe, Potawatomi, and Odawa people. It may also include the Cree, in that the Cree are related to the Council Fires people, although they are not technically Anishinaabe. (Ojibwe)

Chi-miigwech [cheh mee-gwech]: Thank you very much (Ojibwe)

Gunalchéesh [gun-ash CHEESH]: Thank you (Tlingit)

Mni wiconi [miNEE wee-CHOH-nee]: Water is life (Lakota)

Niiji [nee-GEE]: Friend (Ojibwe)

Nokomis [NOO-ko-miss]: Grandmother (Ojibwe)

ILLUSTRATOR'S NOTE

*M*ni wiconi. Water is life. Raised on the beaches and rain forests of Southeast Alaska—home to the Tlingit, Haida, and Tsimshian tribes—I was taught that life is inextricably tied to water. Whether it's the ebb and flow of the ocean or the abundant rainfall that nourishes the lush forests, the spirit of mni wiconi runs through our veins, as it runs through the veins of many people around the world. This is a universal idea that connects all living things. We can all be Water Protectors, caring for each other and protecting our sacred Mother Earth.

The stand at Standing Rock was historic; I was deeply inspired by this solidarity and wanted the illustrations to convey kinship and unity while also representing a diverse group of Indigenous Nations and allies.

To honor Carole's Ojibwe culture, I included several details. For instance, our main protagonist changes into her traditional ribbon skirt as she rallies her people. Additionally, many of the animals included in the book reflect Anishinaabe/Ojibwe clan symbols or hold special significance in traditional teachings, while the repeated floral designs were inspired by traditional Anishinaabe woodland floral motifs.

Standing Rock is just one powerful example of what happens when we rise up, resist, and join together in solidarity for Mother Earth regardless of where we come from. She needs our compassion, love, and respect, and she needs our voices now more than ever. Carole, gunalchéesh for your story. I am deeply honored to have played a role. Gunalchéesh to the Standing Rock Water Protectors for defending the sacred. You are an inspiration to many.

EARTH STEWARD
AND
WATER PROTECTOR
PLEDGE

I will do my best to honor Mother Earth and all its living beings, including the water
and land. I will always remember to treat the Earth as I would like to be treated.

I will treat . . .

the winged ones,

the crawling ones,

the four-legged,

the two-legged,

the plants,

trees,

rivers,

lakes,

the Earth

with kindness and respect.

I pledge to make this world a better place by being a steward of the
Earth and a protector of the water.

_____

My Name

_____

Today's Date